# Postman Pat® and the Greendale Rocket

SIMON AND SCHUSTER

"Mr Pringle says the station hasn't been used for years and years," said Julian excitedly when he got home. "I'm going to write a letter to my pen pal Meera in Pencaster and tell her all about it."

"I remember your Granddad talking about the station and a train, too," sighed Pat. "It used to bring the post in from Pencaster. I bet it's in a right old state now."

The old train station *was* in a terrible state. Paint was peeling, doors were hanging off their hinges, windows were broken and weeds were growing everywhere! "It looks like it's a station for spiders now," said Lucy. The children started to explore. Julian, Katy and Tom ran up to a ramshackle shed.

"I wonder what's in there?" said Julian, peering through a gap in the door.

When they prised open the doors the children saw a large, rusting steam train. Julian chipped away the rust around the nameplate.

"*The Greendale Rocket.* I bet it's the mail train my Dad told me about," he whispered.

On the way home the children met Pat and Ted. They quickly told the pair about their discovery. Ted was almost as excited as they were.

"Come on Pat, let's take a look!" he cried, rushing off to the station.

Finally both the train and the station were finished. Everyone stood on the newly-painted platform with its hanging baskets full of flowers.

Pat proudly released the brake.

*Whooooossshhh!* went the steam but the train didn't move.

"Oh no!" cried Julian. "It's not working."
Pat and Julian walked home sadly. "I'm sorry lad," said Pat.
"I don't know what's wrong with her."
"It's the Grand Opening of the train line next week," replied Julian, "what are we going to do if the train isn't working?"

"What we need is someone who really knows about trains," sighed Pat.

Julian had an idea.

The next morning as Pat and Ted walked onto the station platform they heard a strange banging noise coming from the Greendale Rocket.

"Hello," called Pat nervously.

A head popped out from the cab. "Hello!" it replied. "I'm Ajay."

Ajay explained that he was Meera's father. Julian had written to Meera telling her about the Greendale Rocket.

"He knew I was mad about trains, you see," continued Ajay. "And I think I've found the problem," he added, pointing at the engine.

"Welcome aboard!" said Pat.

The storm had blown itself out and it was bright and sunny for the Grand Opening. As the Greendale Rocket chuffed to a halt on the station platform Pat thanked everyone for their hard work. Best of all, he went on to announce that Ajay and his family were moving to Greendale to help run the Greendale Light Railway.

The whole village cheered as Pat cut the ribbon in front of the train.
"All aboard for the Greendale Rocket!" he cried.

# Postman Pat®'s
# Magic Christmas

SIMON AND SCHUSTER

At the Post Office Mrs Goggins gave Pat a huge pile of parcels and
Christmas cards.
Pat was right. It *was* going to be a busy day! His first delivery was to the
train station. Pat handed Ajay a huge box.
"Oh good, I've been waiting for this," said Ajay, taking a large Christmas
wreath out of the box. He carefully placed it on the front of the
Greendale Rocket. "Ahhh, perfect," he sighed. "I wouldn't want her to
miss out on the festivities."

"I wish it would snow," moaned Julian. "I want to make a snowman.
I wonder if Santa even got my letter?"
"We don't need snow to build a snowman," said Katy Pottage.
The children built a scarecrow snowman instead.

Julian found the stranger's red-and-white hat and put it on the scarecrow's head.
"There you go," said Julian. "He's the best no-snowman ever!"
Soon it was time to go home.

Pat and the stranger were on their way home too when, suddenly, "Ooo-errrr, help!" cried Pat. The van slipped and slithered on a muddy patch of a road, sending them into a field. Pat got out to look and stepped straight into a muddy puddle.

"Here, you can borrow these," said the stranger, handing Pat a pair of big black boots. "I usually carry a spare pair." Together they dug the van out of the mud and were soon on their way again.

It was getting dark and Pat still had letters to deliver. All of Greendale was decorated with Christmas lights. It looked beautiful.

"I'm going to be late for the party," worried Pat. "I won't have time to change."

"Merry Christmas Santa," said Sara, putting a piece of cake and a glass of juice beside the fireplace. "Come on, Julian!" she called. "Let's go to the party."

Everyone thought that Pat had pretended to be Santa.
"Nice one Pat," laughed Ajay, noticing Pat's big black boots.
"Och yes, Pat!" chortled Mrs Goggins. "You made a fine Father Christmas."
Pat was confused. So was Julian.

"If Dad was pretending to be Santa, where's the real Santa?" he asked. "Santa's so busy on Christmas Eve that he has helpers like Daddy," Sara explained. Julian was sad. He thought the *real* Santa had come to the party.

That night, as he lay in bed, Julian heard a strange jingling sound
from downstairs. He went to investigate. And who was there,
putting presents under the tree? Santa!
"Santa, it's really you," cried Julian.
Pat and Sara joined Julian in the doorway.
"Ho, ho, hello Julian. I hope you like the boots, Pat," said Santa,
"and Sara, this cake is delicious."

Before they could answer Santa had disappeared with
a jingling of bells.
"Ho ho. And I've left an extra present for you outside,"
twinkled Santa's voice.

They rushed to the front door.
"Snow!" cried Julian. "It's snowing."
And it was! Beautiful, thick, white snow covered Greendale.
"Thank you, Santa!" called Julian.
A bright light whizzed across the sky like a shooting star.
"Ho, ho, ho! Merry Christmas everyone," laughed Santa.

# Postman Pat®
# Clowns Around

SIMON AND SCHUSTER

The circus was coming to Greendale and the children were very excited.

"I'm going to be in a circus when I grow up!" announced Bill Thompson.

"You have to be good at something to be in a circus," joked Meera.

"You can be good at anything if you work at it!" Bill laughed as he ran over to see Pat.

Back home, Pat got on the phone to Julia Pottage.

"I'll be picking the tent up from the station tomorrow," Pat told her. "So, we'll meet on the village green in the morning. Spread the word, Julia, we'll need plenty of help! Right, Jess, we're all set!"

"Miaow!"

The next morning, Pat delivered the post to Nisha. "Ajay's got the tent for the circus, Pat," she told him.

"Oh great! The children will be thrilled. And Reverend Timms – you're just the man we need. Could you help us with the music for the circus?"

"Circus? Music?" asked the vicar. "Well… I'm not really very good, but, well, why not, it'll be a challenge! I'd better get started straight away!"

Pat and Ajay struggled with the big tent. "Phew!" gasped Ajay. "It's heavy!"

"You're not kidding!" wheezed Pat.

They staggered along the platform and over the bridge. The tent was too big to fit in the van, so poor old Pat and Ajay had to carry it all the way to the village green. The villagers cheered.

"Well done, Pat! Keep going, Ajay!"

Meanwhile, the Reverend Timms was rummaging about in the vestry cupboard.

"Now then, let me see… oh, a trumpet!"

Clouds of dust poured out as he gave the trumpet a quick toot.

"And here's my old gramophone! That will do nicely… and aha! Just the job! My one-man-band outfit. Perfect!"

BOOM PAPAAH, BOOM BANG-A-BANG…

The vicar marched up and down until CRASH! he toppled over.

Tom, Katy, Charlie and Sarah were practising their bean-bag juggling.
"Come on," said Charlie, "juggling is easy. One, two, three, GO!"
The bean bags went flying all over the place.

"You're doing it all wrong!" said Bill. "I'll show you."

He flung the beanbags up into the air, and they fell straight back onto his head.

"I don't want to juggle anyway," Bill muttered, as the others burst out laughing.

Back on the village green, PC Selby and Alf were having a spot of bother with the tent.

Dorothy and Julia were doing their best to help.

"Ready? Pull!"

"To the right, no, to the left . . ."

"Keep pulling… that's it…"

"No! Too far!"

"Oops! Look out!"

The pole teetered over and the tent collapsed in a heap. Alf, Pat and PC Selby just managed to escape in time!

"Come on everyone," encouraged Pat. "We can do it!"

With a lot of heaving and huffing and hammering, the tent was finally up.

Nisha and Sarah arrived with tea and cakes. "Well done, everyone! Time for a break!"

Pat was sipping his tea when he saw Bill sitting on the bench next to the green. He looked miserable. Jess was trying to cheer him up.

"Miaow?"

"What's up, Bill?" asked Pat.

"I can't do anything!" Bill wailed. "All I can do is make people laugh!"

"It's good to make people laugh," smiled Pat. "And it's just given me an idea!"

By the evening, the big top was ready and it was time for the circus!

The audience were in their seats.

The Reverend Timms gave a dramatic drum roll ...

and in strode Jeff Pringle, dressed in top hat and red coat.

"Ladies and gentlemen! Welcome to the Greendale Circus. Let the show begin!"

The bean-bag jugglers were brilliant...

The rhythmic ribbon dancers were stunning...

And Jess the lion performed perfectly!

But the real stars
of the show were
Pat and Bill
Thompson, the
funniest circus
clowns ever.

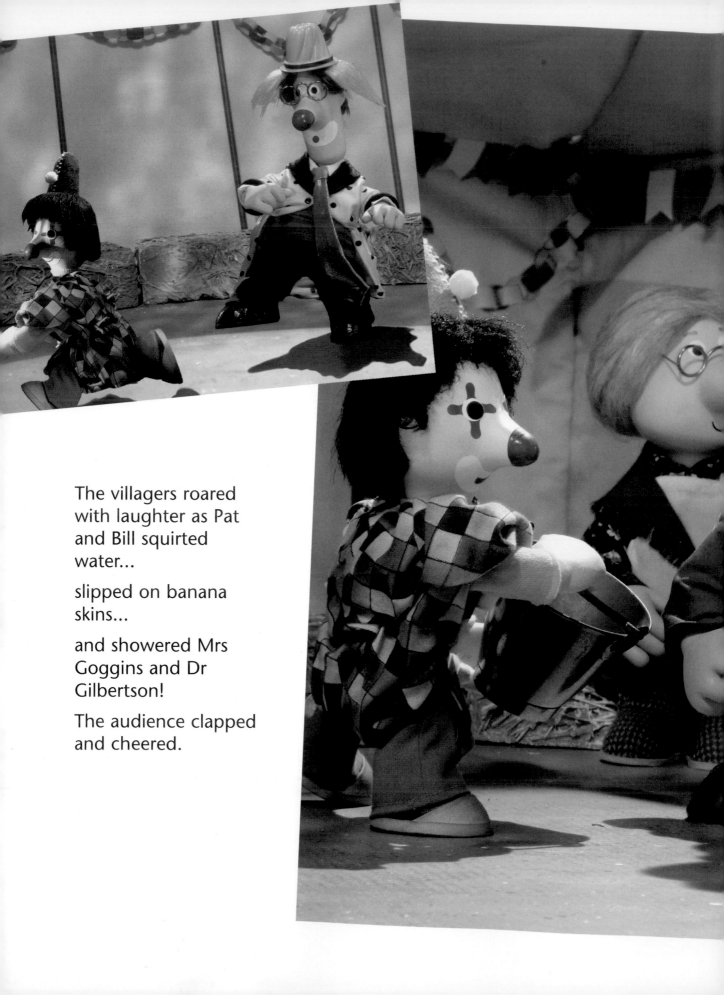

The villagers roared with laughter as Pat and Bill squirted water...

slipped on banana skins...

and showered Mrs Goggins and Dr Gilbertson!

The audience clapped and cheered.

"Ladies and gentlemen," shouted Jeff above the applause. "Thank you for coming to the Greendale Circus. Three cheers for our talented children – and an extra one for the clowns! Hip Hip Hooray!"